W9-CKL-862

METEOR!

METEOR!

PATRICIA POLACCO

G.P. Putnam's Sons
New York

To my family—who actually lived this remarkable event.

G. P. Putnam's Sons, a division of The Putnam & Grosset Group,
200 Madison Avenue, New York, NY 10016.
Sandcastle Books and the Sandcastle logo are trademarks
belonging to The Putnam & Grosset Group.
First Sandcastle Books edition, 1992.
Originally published in 1987 by Dodd, Mead & Company, New York.
Published simultaneously in Canada.
Printed in Hong Kong.
Book design by Barbara DuPree Knowles.

Library of Congress Cataloging-in-Publication Data
Polacco, Patricia. Meteor! Summary: A quiet rural
community is dramatically changed when a meteor
crashes down in the front yard of the Gaw family.
[1. Meteors—Fiction   2. Country life—Fiction]
I. Title. [PZ7.P75186Me 1988] [E] 88-23895
ISBN 0-399-21699-5 (hardcover)
10 9 8 7 6 5
ISBN 0-399-22407-6 (Sandcastle)
10 9 8 7 6 5 4 3 2

Many years ago, when
my brother and I were small, Mom
let us spend the summer with
our Gramma and Grampa Gaw
on their farm in Michigan.

One night, far above that little
farm, a star sputtered and
flashed and started to fall.

As it fell through the night sky, the geese honked their alarm, the chickens cackled, and the goats bleated and jumped wildly about.

The bright light with a long fiery tail streaked through the sky unnoticed by my family. Grampa was reading the Herald, Gramma was correcting school papers, Cousin Steve was tinkering with his wireless, my brother Richard was practicing the piano, and I was reading a storybook.

Suddenly, without warning, the house started shaking.
Plaster came loose from the ceiling. Dishes fell from shelves.
Rugs curled on the floor as if they had a life of their own.

The flaming object made a terrible sound as it went shrieking
over the roof of the house. Then it crashed into the ground with a
horribly loud BOOM. It landed with such force that glass broke,
chairs overturned, windows rattled, and walls shuddered.

The front door was laid open by the blast and through it an eerie light could be seen glowing from a big hole in the front yard. We were stunned. But soon curiosity overcame caution and we timidly made our way outdoors for a look-see.

"Why, it's a fallen star!" Grampa gasped.

"Of all the places on earth a meteor could have fallen, it landed smack-dab in the middle of our yard," Gramma exclaimed.

Grampa and Cousin Steve pounded stakes all around the meteor and roped it off.

The next morning Gramma called Uncle Carl. "That's what I said, Carl, a real falling star, right in my front yard."

Carl called Bertie Potter. "Did you hear, Bertie, a falling star, out by the Gaw place in Mudsock Meadow. Came in so low it almost hit the house."

Bertie called Mayor Hatch. "That's right, Howard, it took off the roof, and almost hit the clothes line. That poor family."

Mayor Hatch called Pearlie Beach. "Unbelievable! Took the roof, the power lines, and hit a cow!"

Pearlie called Vera. "I tell ya . . . it flattened
the Gaw place, took the power lines, water mains,
killed the stock, and it's still smoking."

Vera called Mr. Titus at the hardware store.
"The whole place is gone, the barn, the animals,
and there's poison smoke a-comin' from it."

Mr. Titus called Officer Washburn, who called the Fire Chief.
"Sounds like they'll be needin' us," Chief Quisle exclaimed.
He started up Engine 23, turned on the siren, and headed out.

But news traveled through town faster than
the engine could leave the firehouse . . .

. . . and Union City was A-BUZZ with what had happened in Mudsock Meadow. Merchants closed their shops, school was let out before noon, and just about everyone in town headed for the Gaw place to see the mysterious meteor.

"I wonder how big it is?"

"Just think, it came from way out in space!"

"Isn't this the most excitin' thing . . . I can't wait
to see Carlie, George, and the kids."

"This is more excitin' than when Bertie Felspaw
got her elbow caught in the revolving door
at the library over Coldwater way!"

As the crowd jostled, trotted, rolled, and bumped through the countryside, bystanders and onlookers joined in and came along to see the meteor. Dr. Trotter's Medicine Wagon, the Coldwater Chautauqua Circus, and the Union City Ladies Lyceum fell in with the parade of citizens. They were soon joined by the Union City High School band which hooted, tooted, boomed, and jingled their instruments as they ran down the hillside.

As more and more people arrived, Gramma and Grampa's farm soon became a carnival of *meteoric* events. *Meteor* basket lunches were auctioned, *meteor* popcorn was popped, *meteor* lemonade was made, *meteor* liniment was sold, and the Chautauqua Circus was going to give a *meteoric* performance.

But most folks simply stood and stared at the wondrous meteor. "To think," Gramma repeated to everyone, "of all the places on earth it could have landed, it came smack-dab in the middle of our yard!" She beamed with pride and was truly happy to see friends that she usually only saw once or twice a year.

Heleo the Great, Master of Stratospheric Maneuvers and Atmospheric Acrobatics (while on his way to the Ionia State Fair) landed his hot air balloon and offered special *meteor* rides. These included an ascent of approximately forty feet and a slow descent in order to take in the full panorama of the farm and the meteor.

The Union City High School band gave a *meteoric* concert.

In the midst of all the festivities a group of scientists arrived from Battle Creek College, The University of Michigan, and Michigan State University science departments. They set up all their buzzing, testing equipment and put on strange-looking protective suits.

They turned on all of the machinery. CLICK . . . . . CLICK . . . . . POP . . . . . WHIZZZZZZZ, PEWPRY . . . . . PEWPRY, it went.

The scientists looked thoughtful, scratched their heads, and wrote down lots and lots of data. They measured, pondered, quizzed, and figured. The crowd leaned closer as their chief finally spoke. . . . "Yes, sir! That there is a genuine meteorite!"

The crowd clapped and cheered. Charlie Lake struck up the band, and the circus began a *meteoric* performance.

Ling Po and Ping How, the jugglers, threw little golden balls and shiny silver rings around and around in the air, while Tilly and Lilly, the dancing elephants balanced on one foot as the "Leaping Luckies," the trained dogs, jumped about and did somersaults.

The Union City Lyceum dance troupe performed a special number of interpretive movement depicting both the falling of the meteor and the last days of Pompei.

"I touched the meteor," Tommy Enderby said to Marietta Krimmel, "and as soon as I did, I could play my trumpet better than ever before!"

Marietta told Cecile Potter that after she touched the meteor, she thought up the best recipe for pie she ever did have. "I'm gonna enter the pie contest at the next fair," she exclaimed.

Cecile told Dr. Trotter that since she'd touched the meteor she had more energy than she'd had in years. "I tell ya, I could feel something coming right up into my finger from that there fallen star. It's magic, I tell ya."

Dr. Trotter claimed that ever since he touched the meteor, his liniment had acquired super-mysterious healing powers.

Hollis D. Lonsberry, in turn, was convinced that his best hog was going to become a prize winner. "I'm gonna enter him in the Ionia State Fair," he chirped to Gladys Pardee.

Gladys was positive that since she touched the meteor her eyesight improved instantly. "I'm tellin' yer, Leonard," she said to Mr. Pinehurst, "I can see all the way across the barnyard!"

"Extraordinary," he sighed, as he stared at his forefinger. "I touched it too, and I feel special, REALLY SPECIAL!"

As folks left the Gaw farm that day they all felt special. They were changed somehow, inspired by the act of touching something that had flown across the galaxy.

It seemed like magic all right. The Union City High School band went on to win the State Championship that year, thanks to a trumpet solo played by Tommy Enderby, and Marietta's currant-blueberry pie took first place at the county fair. Hollis D. Lonsberry's best hog, Herman, won Best-of-Show at the Iona State Fair.

Maybe these things would have happened anyway—but who can say for sure? All I know is that for three generations the meteor was a source of wonder to the little town of Union City, Michigan, and especially to my family.

It remained on the very spot where it landed until it was moved to a lovely green hillside overlooking the St. Joseph River to become my grandmother's headstone. It is there to this day!

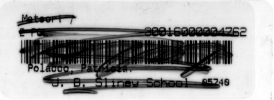